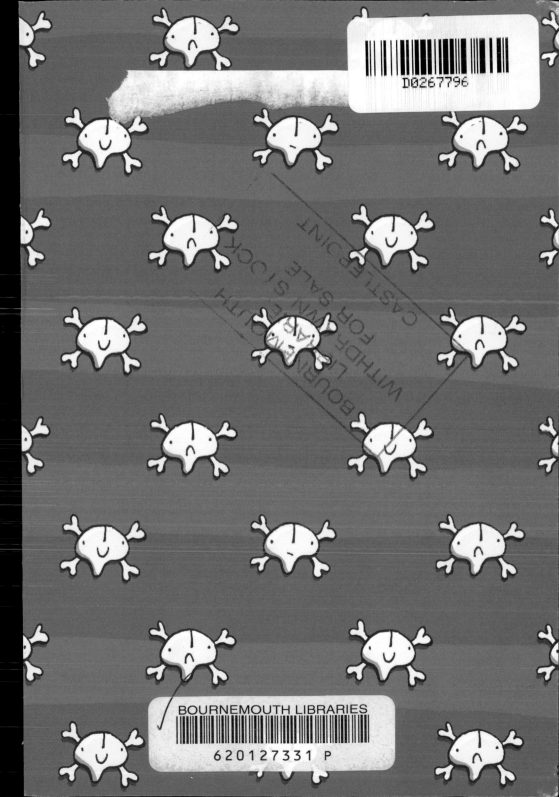

Pirate Patch

and the

Great Sea Chase

In which the proud Pirate Patch and his cousin Poppy quit quarrelling and together defeat the villianous Bones and Jones

For Jasmine
R.I.

For Christina
N.R.

Reading Consultant: Prue Goodwin, Lecturer in Literacy and
Children's Books at the University of Reading

ORCHARD BOOKS
338 Euston Road, London NW1 3BH
Orchard Books Australia
Hachette Children's Books
Level 17/207 Kent Street, Sydney NSW 2000

First published by Orchard Books in 2009

A CIP catalogue record for this book is available from the British Library

ISBN 978 1 84362 979 5 (hardback)
ISBN 978 1 84362 987 0 (paperback)

1 3 5 7 9 10 8 6 4 2 (hardback)
1 3 5 7 9 10 8 6 4 2 (paperback)
Printed in China

Orchard Books is a division of Hachette Children's Books,
an Hachette Livre UK company.
www.hachettelivre.co.uk

Pirate Patch
and the
Great Sea Chase

ROSE IMPEY ❖ NATHAN REED

ORCHARD BOOKS

Patch and Granny Peg were
in a bad mood, and it was all
because of the letter.

Patch's cousin, Poppy, was
coming to stay for a few days.
Patch thought Poppy was
the bossiest girl he had ever met.

And Poppy thought Patch was the most big-headed boy *she* had ever met.

The moment the two set sail together, there was always trouble. Anything Patch could do, Poppy could do better . . .

and bigger . . .

and faster . . .

They always argued about who should be in charge, but in the end Patch always won.

Today their arguments were giving Peg a headache. She decided to go and lie down in a dark cabin. Pierre and Portside went too.

Patch and Poppy hardly noticed.
They were too busy fighting
over the ship's compass . . .

and the telescope . . .

and the map!

In no time *The Little Pearl* was
sailing off course.
But Patch and Poppy were
too busy fighting to notice.

Suddenly Patch did notice another ship heading towards them. It was his enemies: the *villainous* Bones and Jones!

"Quick," he said. "Let's get out of here." Patch steered the ship the way Poppy had been pointing. "Told you so," she said, smugly.

The Little Pearl was racing flat out, but *The Black Bonnet* soon caught up with her.

"I know what to do," Poppy told Patch. "Sail in a figure of eight. We'll soon lose them."

Patch wanted to ignore Poppy . . .
but he didn't have a better plan.
And Poppy's plan seemed to work.
"Told you so," she said, smugly.

In no time *The Black Bonnet*
caught up again.
"I know what to do," Poppy told
Patch. "Head for that sand bank.
We'll soon lose them."

Patch wanted to ignore Poppy . . .
but he didn't have a better plan.
And Poppy's plan seemed to work.
"Told you so!" she said, smugly.

But before long Bones and Jones
caught up *again.*
"I know," Poppy told Patch.
"Head for one of those coves.
We'll soon lose them."

Patch *almost* ignored Poppy . . . but at the last minute he raced his ship into a small cove.

Before Poppy could smile her smug smile, *The Black Bonnet* was right behind them again!

This time Patch had his own plan.

He steered *The Little Pearl* into the
gap between two *huge* rocks.
Poppy was sure they were going
to crash!

But it was Patch's turn to smile.
Maybe his little ship wasn't as
fast as *The Black Bonnet*, but she
wasn't as *fat* either!

The Little Pearl sailed through the gap. But the big, fat *Black Bonnet* was stuck fast.

Later, when the rest of the crew came on deck, they had no idea what adventures they'd missed.

For the rest of the trip Patch and Poppy were *very* polite to one other. "After you," insisted Patch. "No, after *you*," insisted Poppy.

It was all beginning to make
Granny Peg very nervous.

"Did you have a good time with cousin Poppy?" Mum and Dad asked Patch.

"Not really," said Patch. "Girls are far too bossy for my liking!"

Peg gave a sigh of relief.
Everything seemed back
to normal at last.

★ Pirate Patch ★

Rose Impey   Nathan Reed

All priced at £8.99

Orchard Colour Crunchies are available from all good bookshops,
or can be ordered direct from the publisher:
Orchard Books, PO BOX 29, Douglas IM99 1BQ
Credit card orders please telephone 01624 836000
or fax 01624 837033 or visit our internet site: www.orchardbooks.co.uk
or e-mail: bookshop@enterprise.net for details.

To order please quote title, author and ISBN
and your full name and address.
Cheques and postal orders should be made payable to 'Bookpost plc.'
Postage and packing is FREE within the UK
(overseas customers should add £2.00 per book).

Prices and availability are subject to change.

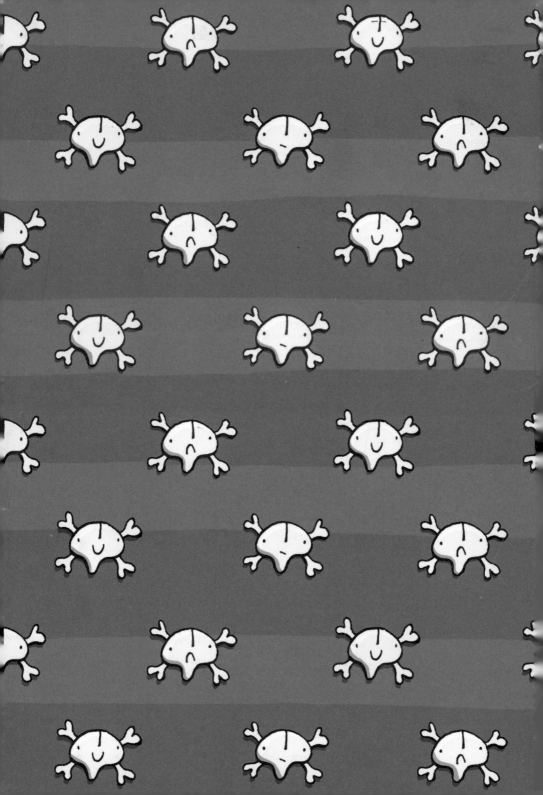